This Little Hippo
book belongs to

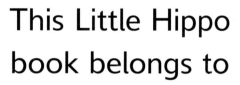

_____

_____

Scholastic Children's Books,
Commonwealth House, 1-19 New Oxford Street,
London WC1A 1NU, UK
a division of Scholastic Ltd

London ~ New York ~ Toronto ~ Sydney ~ Auckland

First published by Scholastic Ltd, 1998

Copyright © 1998 Link Licensing Ltd/Hibbert Ralph Entertainment
Licensed by Link Licensing Ltd

Developed from the original book The Night After Christmas,
by James Stevenson. The Forgotten Toys is an animated series produced
by Hibbert Ralph Entertainment for Link Entertainment,
scripted by Mark Holloway,
directed by Graham Ralph and produced by Karen Davidsen.
Executive producers David Hamilton and Claire Derry.
Script adaptation by Norman Redfern. Book illustrations by Les Gibbard.
All rights reserved.

2 4 6 8 10 9 7 5 3 1

ISBN 0 590 19977 3

Printed in Belgium by Proost

The Forgotten Toys

Hospital Toys

Once upon a time, when they were far away from home,
a little girl and her brother lost their favourite toys . . . and the
toys didn't like being lost. Now Teddy, and Annie the ragdoll,
were on their way home, but the journey back to their children
was long and full of adventures.

Teddy and Annie were standing outside a big shop. Teddy was playing with the automatic doors. When he walked towards them, they opened. When he walked away, they closed.

"Open says me!" he commanded.

"It's 'Open Sesame'," Annie told him.

"No, it isn't," argued Teddy. "Look – open says me!"

As if by magic, the doors opened.

"Can't catch me, says me!" said Teddy.

"Teddy! Someone's coming!" warned Annie.

Teddy stood still, and the doors closed on him. He was trapped.

"Come on," said Annie.

"I can't!" squealed Teddy.

Annie grabbed Teddy by the arm and pulled him free. But his other arm was stuck in the door. The automatic doors opened again to let in a customer, and Teddy snatched back his missing arm.

"I'll sew it back on for you," said Annie.

"No you won't," snapped Teddy. "This is an emergency.
I should be in hospital!"
He handed the arm to Annie and limped painfully away.
Around the corner, Teddy spotted an ambulance.

"Come on!" he shouted, running towards the open doors.

"Are you sure you need it?" asked Annie. "You look much
better all of a sudden."

Teddy and Annie hid inside the ambulance. They watched as a little girl was carried in on a stretcher. Her name was Flora.

"She looks sad," said Annie. "I wish I could help her."

Annie moved a little closer to Flora. The little girl picked her up and held her tight as the ambulance raced through the streets to the hospital. She was still cuddling Annie when they carried her inside.

"What about me?" Teddy complained. "I'm the emergency."
He jumped out of the ambulance and chased after Flora's trolley.
   "Pigtails! Come back!" he shouted.
   "I can't," said Annie. "Catch!"
She threw Teddy's arm towards him.

"How can I catch with only one arm?" said Teddy.
His arm landed on the floor, but before he could reach it, a
floor-polisher whisked it away. Teddy ran after it. He rescued
his arm, but as he tried to escape he collided with the
fast-moving polisher.

It spun him away across the corridor, through a door and smack into a bowl full of plaster. Teddy struggled to his feet. The plaster was already beginning to set.

"I'm stuck!" he shouted. "Pigtails!"

But Annie couldn't hear him. She was tucked up in bed next to Flora, and Flora wanted her mummy.

"Don't worry," said Annie, "she's with the doctor. I'll look after you."

"You can talk!" exclaimed Flora.

"Yes," said Annie, "but don't tell anyone."

"Why are you in hospital?" Flora asked.

"My friend Teddy, he's a bear. His arm came off. We came to have it sewn back on again," explained Annie.

"I'm having my tonsils out," said Flora. "They really hurt."

"Don't worry," said Annie. "You'll feel better soon."

"I know I'll be all right if you stay with me," said Flora.

"I will," promised Annie.

Staff Nurse Scrubbitt had never seen such a messy bear. First she chipped off the plaster, then she washed him, and then she hung him up to dry.

"That will do for now," she said. "You'll make a wonderful present for one of the children. There's a little girl who'd love you." As soon as the nurse had gone, Teddy unpegged his arm and launched himself into the air. He landed in the sink. Teddy reached for the taps and hauled himself out again.

"Right," he said, "all I need now is a doctor!"

13

The doctor already had a patient to look after.

"Time to take out those tonsils, Flora," he said.

"Can Annie come too?" Flora asked him.

"No, she doesn't need an operation," replied Doctor Pulse.

"Her friend, Teddy, does," said Flora.

"Well, she'd better send him to me," said the doctor.

Flora turned back to say goodbye to Annie.

"You will be here when I come back? Promise?" she asked.

"I'll be here," Annie promised.

Teddy was looking for someone to sew back his arm. He spotted some people in white coats.

"They look like doctors," he said.
He followed them into a room where some strange operations were going on. Some of the people in white coats were chopping, and some were slicing . . .

"Hold on," he muttered, "I don't like the look of those doctors! It's not safe in here."

Teddy ran out of the kitchen and jumped aboard a passing linen trolley, which he hoped would take him to a nicer kind of doctor. Annie was waiting in Flora's bed. She was worried about Teddy, but she knew that she had promised to be there when Flora came back.

"Teddy can look after himself," she thought. "No, he can't. I'll find him and then come back here again."

She climbed out of bed and began searching for him. The linen trolley was at the top of the laundry chute. The nurse tipped it forwards, and all the dirty linen fell down the chute.

Teddy tumbled out, caught hold of the top of the chute, but couldn't stop his arm from falling.

"Help!" he shouted. "Where's Pigtails? Typical doll – never there when you need her!"

Annie heard Teddy's cry for help. She rushed to the laundry chute and leaned over. Teddy was still hanging on, but when he grabbed her hand they both fell in. Together they fell, and fell, and fell, until they landed in a pile of sheets at the bottom. Teddy picked up his arm.

"Haven't you had that put back yet?" asked Annie. "You need
to see a doctor."

"I've seen loads of doctors," said Teddy, "but they haven't seen me."

"Let's go and find one who will," suggested Annie.

Annie led Teddy to the operating theatre.

"This is where the doctors make people better," she explained.

"What about toys?" asked Teddy.

"And toys, I hope," said Annie. "Anyway, it's a good place to start." They went into a room full of surgical instruments. Teddy picked up a surgeon's mask and tried it on. Next, he found a silver bowl, and put it on his head.

"Vroom, vroom! I'm a racing-driver doctor!" he shouted, and began racing up and down. Pills, bandages and instruments clattered to the floor.

"You'll break something," warned Annie. "I'm going back to wait for Flora. I promised I'd be there."

She left the room. Alone again, Teddy realised that he had lost his arm. He started looking through the bandages, but the more he searched, the more mess he made. Suddenly, the door opened, and Doctor Pulse and Nurse Scrubbit wheeled in Flora.

"What's been going on in here?" asked Nurse Scrubbitt.
She picked Teddy up and gave him to Flora.

"Here's a teddy for you, dear," she said.

"He must be Annie's friend," said Flora. "You said you'd help him."
Doctor Pulse picked up Teddy's arm.

"So I did," he said. "We'll do our best for him."

When Flora got back to her bed, she found Annie waiting for her. Flora was happy, but Annie was sad and worried.

"Teddy lost his arm and now he can't find it," said Annie. "I should never have left him on his own."

"It's all right," said Flora. "Look!"

Doctor Pulse and Nurse Scrubbitt were bringing in another patient.
He had two arms, and he was snoring.
Teddy woke up. His arm was as good as new.

"I wish you could stay with me for ever," said Flora.

"We've got our own children," said Annie. "We just need to find them again. We'd better be going."

"Look," said Teddy. "Who's that coming?"
Flora's family arrived.

Flora's parents had brought her a present. It was a new doll. She didn't notice Annie and Teddy climb out of her bed, but as she hugged her new doll, she saw them waving goodbye from the doorway. She waved back, but they were gone. They were on their way home.